REX²

Book #2 in the TIME SOLDIERS® Series

Creator & Photographer
ROBERT GOULD

Digital Illustrator
EUGENE EPSTEIN

Writers
KATHLEEN DUEY & ROBERT GOULD

5:14 AM

The swirling light had led to quiet woods…
a perfect place to dig a nest. But now, T-Rex
could smell the small, dangerous invaders
that had attacked the day before.

The egg could be in danger unless they were
destroyed!

The scent-trail led to a hard, black path and
the strangest place T-Rex had ever seen.

Jon was startled awake by the sound of heavy breathing.

He sat up in bed, hoping it was a dream. It wasn't.

Next door, Rob and Mikey awakened to a rattling of their windows.

The Tyrannosaurus stalked around the house. It was looking for a way to get in.

Across the street, Mariah grabbed the phone and called 911. "There's a Tyrannosaurus Rex—" she began.

"We handle *real* emergencies," the operator interrupted.

"It's true!" Mariah insisted. "Please, send help!"

Mariah didn't see the big black truck parked at the top of the hill. She didn't know that a tall man in a dark suit had intercepted her call.

She couldn't hear the harsh, hypersonic squeal of his top-secret equipment.

But Rex could...and it was painful.
The dinosaur ran to get away from the

The neighbors were all fast asleep, except
one, the new kid in the neighborhood.

"We have to do something!" Rob said, dressing as fast as he could.

"Mikey, go get the videocam from the clubhouse. It's hanging on the wall."

A minute later, Mikey came back frowning. "Rob...the tape...it's gone."

Rob took the camera and flipped open the side panel. "Oh no!"

Rex was angry and confused. Why would this infuriating red animal *refuse* to get out of the way? A hard nudge had scared it and it began to call, a terrible wailing cry that seemed endless. Rex placed one foot on its back and pressed down...hard.

The ear-splitting cry stopped.

Stepping around the defeated animal, Rex looked down the wide, black path and saw a huge lake. The water was moving. Curious, Rex saw more creatures in a strange hollow place as big as the biggest rocks in her valley. Strong smells came on the wind...water and salt, mixed with the scents of fire and scorching meat.

A sudden commotion in the parking lot startled Rex. There were more hard-skinned animals like the red one with the loud cry. rows of

Whirling to face them, Rex's tail smashed into the hollow place. The creatures trapped inside screamed and ran to escape. Rex turned

Rex waded in cautiously. Overhead, a noisy flying animal buzzed just out of reach.

Some of the small, dangerous creatures

They worried Rex. How many of them *were* there? Would they find the egg?

The Time Soldiers were geared up and ready to go. "What's the plan?" Adam asked.

Rob shrugged. "I'm not sure yet. First, we have to find the Tyrannosaurus." He glanced back. An unfamiliar black truck was parked up the hill. It was huge…big enough to haul a T-Rex.

"Let's go!" Jon said.

They flew downhill, cornering hard at the intersection.

LIVE RGtv 10

The RG-TV news team was at the restaurant within minutes. Rod Luck and his camera crew linked to anchorwoman Denise Fuller.

"We take you now to an incredible scene," she told her audience. "What appears to be a living dinosaur...a Tyrannosaurus Rex...is making its way north on the beach."

Jon got the first look. "It's headed for the oil storage tanks," he yelled.

He scowled, shaking his head. "Oh, no... an oil truck."

Another noisy, flying animal circled over-head. Rex was puzzled. The tree trunks were the right shape, but they were smooth and white and smelled wrong. A big orange

It sounded a deafening challenge as it moved closer. Rex attacked, ripping the enemy's skin. Strange, smelly blood sprayed out, then burst into flames. Rex was desperate to escape the

Adam pulled out his binoculars. "The Tyrannosaurus wrecked the tanker truck," he said. "Wow! Now it's thrashing the whole area. Oh, man...there it goes!"

"Which way?" Jon demanded.

Adam lowered the binoculars. "Straight for the highway."

Rob pointed. "OK, if we can get up the hill fast enough, maybe we can warn the drivers."

"How?" Jon asked.

Rob shook his head. "I don't know, but we have to try."

They pedaled hard. But it was too late.

Rex hated the wailing of the charging animals on the hard black path. It was impossible to fight them all.

There was no choice but to keep running.

On the hilltop, a field of flowers spread in every direction. It was quiet, until the buzzing throb of the flying animal

Rex retreated, frantic to get away from it.

"Can you see it?" Rob asked Adam.

Adam focused the binoculars. "It's headed for the big construction site. Wow! You should see these guys' faces."

"Let's go!" Rob said, climbing back on his bike. "I know a shortcut."

Rex stared. There were several of the big animals and two of the small, dangerous

There was a familiar scent in the air. Had it finally found the creatures it had come

"It sees us," Rob shouted. "We have to create a diversion. That will give those

The T-Rex started after Jon, then switched to chasing Mikey. Mariah cut in close to

The equipment operators ran to safety, grateful for the kids' bravery.

Scrambling into their tractors, they started the engines...determined to help the kids.

The roaring of the hard-skinned animals was awful. Their breath was hot and smelled like fire. Furious, Rex seized a

The small, dangerous creature inside it jumped free and ran. Rex turned to chase it.

Rob stood on his pedals and turned in a tight circle, his back tire sliding. He controlled the skid, then shot forward, shouting to distract the dinosaur.

It spun around, knocking his bike sideways with a flick of its tail. Rob fell hard, sprawling on the dirt.

"Rob!" Mikey screamed.

But before any of them could move, broad wings swooped close to the rampaging T-Rex.

Desperate, Rob jumped, grabbing onto the Quetzalcoatlus as it rose, carrying him to safety.

He dropped to the ground on the ridge top. Looking back toward his astonished friends, he saw something very mysterious...

Tell us how *you* think the Quetzalcoatlus got here and where you think it will finally end up and **YOU COULD WIN A ROLE in an upcoming Time Soldiers book!**

Enter Rob's "Big Bird" Contest at:

www.timesoldiers.com

There was a long black truck pulling up...the same one that had been parked on their street. Two men in dark suits climbed out.

They carried the creepiest-looking weapons Rob had ever seen. He ran toward Mikey and the others.

Without saying a word, the men lifted their strange weapons and fired at the raging Tyrannosaurus.

As the humming green light struck it, the T-Rex roared and began to stagger.

Rob sprinted downhill, then dove behind a giant dozer. "I saw that truck this morning!" he said, breathing hard. "On our street and—"

The ground shook as the T-Rex collapsed. Then, strangely, everything went silent.

The tractor engines had stopped running. The news helicopter had disappeared.

The men in dark suits lowered their weapons and stood looking at the fallen Tyrannosaurus.

Mikey stared at the truck. Whatever was inside it was connected to the time portal, Rex and the missing videotape! He was sure of it.

Mikey suddenly took off toward the truck.

"Stop him, Jon!" Rob shouted. But it was too late.

38

Glancing around, Mikey climbed inside the truck. The metal floor was smooth, almost slick. He stepped forward cautiously. Computer screens glowed with columns of blinking numbers.

And there, placed neatly beside one of the monitors, was their videotape. *Yes!*

Enter Adam's "Men In Dark Suits" Contest at:  www.timesoldiers.com

"Put that back." The voice was cold. Mikey jerked around. One of the strange men was standing there. Mikey gripped the tape tightly. "You *stole* this, he said."

"Just put it back," said the man in the dark suit leaning forward to step up into the truck.

Mikey bolted, darting past him before he could react.

...suddenly he felt an iron grip around his ankle. A second later he heard Rob's voice.

"Let my brother go!"

As Rob's boot slammed down, the grip released and Mikey scrambled to his feet.

He ran faster than he ever had in his life.

"Slingshots!" Rob shouted.

Slingshots at the ready, they faced the angry Tyrannosaurus...but it didn't come toward them.

Mariah pointed. "It's going back to the time portal!"

"Let's go!" Jon said.

They ran for their bikes.

Cutting corners, using every bike path and shortcut they knew, they managed to keep up with Rex...following it into the woods.

"Keep going!" Mikey yelled, swerving off the path. "I'll meet you there!"

He stopped, jumping off his bike to hide the videotape deep into the base of their secret tree. He knew it would be safe *here*.

Near the time portal, Rob braked, astonished. The T-Rex didn't even glance at them. It didn't look fierce anymore. It looked sad and scared.

"Look," Rob said, "an egg. She...*she's* trying to move her egg."

"So it was just —" Jon began.

"—protecting her baby," Rob interrupted. "It's a *mother* dinosaur."

Mikey and Adam glanced at each other, then lowered their heads and stared at the ground.

Mariah kicked at the dirt.

Bernardo wiped his eyes.

The kids stood in silence.

Rex pushed her egg gently into the portal. She looked back once and roared...but it was an entirely different sound than they had ever heard her make before.

"Does she know we understand now?" Jon wondered aloud.

Rob glanced at him. "I hope so." Then he flinched. The men in dark suits were standing behind them. One of them was holding the videotape.

"Give that back," Rob demanded.

Mikey clenched his fists. "How'd you find it?"

The men remained silent. They simply looked at each other, turned around and walked toward the trees.

"Rob, look!" Adam shouted. "In the portal...who is *that?*"

48

Mikey turned to demand the videotape back...but the men in dark suits were nowhere to be seen.

"Look!" Rob shouted.

Jon whirled and stared at the closing portal. He blinked. A pirate? As he tried to focus, a sharp pain in his head startled him. He pressed a hand against his forehead.

"Are you all right?" Rob asked.

Jon nodded. But the pain was weird, a giant headache behind his eyes.

The portal collapsed with a rumble, disappearing in a cloud of dust.

Mikey glanced at Rob, then Jon. "They took our video-tape again. We can't prove anything."

"The portal will open again," Mariah said.

"It has to," Bernardo agreed.

"When?" Adam asked.

No one answered...because no one knew.